# AN IMAGINARY MENAGERIE

Poems and Drawings by
## ROGER McGOUGH

FRANCES LINCOLN
CHILDREN'S BOOKS

# Contents

# Allivator

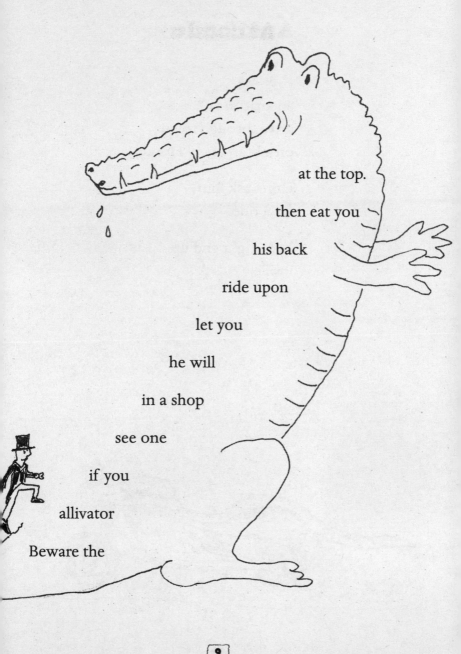

at the top.

then eat you

his back

ride upon

let you

he will

in a shop

see one

if you

allivator

Beware the

# Anaconda

Ever see
an anaconda
drive through town
on a brand new Honda?

Don't ask him
for a ride

You might end up
inside.

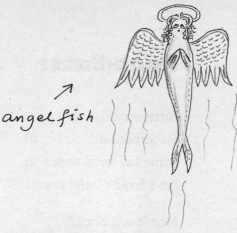

*angelfish*

# Anglefish

Anglefish
are literally
trilateral

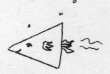

Living
littorally
comes natural

If you see one
near the reef
say hello

But  what big teeth!
Is that a shark
down below?

# Aunt-Eater

Aunt-eater, aunt-eater
Where have you been?
Aunt Liz took you walkies
And hasn't been seen

Nor has Aunt Mary
Aunt Lil or Aunt Di
Aunt-eater, aunt-eater
Why the gleam in your eye?

# Badgers and Goodgers

Once upon a time,
there lived in the forest
Badgers and Goodgers.

Badgers emerged only after dark
using foul language,
and gobbled up all the blind dormice,
deaf bats and lame frogs
they could lay their greasy claws on,
as well as choice morsels of any child
who happened to wander innocently
into the forest, way past its bedtime.

Goodgers, on the other hand,
were bright-eyed and light as marshmallows.
They loved to dance in the sunshine
and could sing in many languages.
When not jogging or clearing litter
they nibbled moon beans and alfresco sprouts
and ate lots of fibre.

And then suddenly, without warning,
there came The Great Drought
followed by The Great Fire
followed by The Great Flood
followed by The Great Plague
followed by The Great Jazz Revival
And when finally The Great Famine
took the forest by the throat

It was the Badgers
who wheeled and dealed
and looted and hoarded.
Who connived, ducked and dived.

And it was the Goodgers
who cared and shared
and helped those
less fortunate than themselves.

Unfortunately,
the less fortunate survived
and the Goodgers perished.
Which just goes to show.

And so when Pan
(The Great Spirit of the Animal Kingdom)
returned to the forest after a fortnight in Portugal
he was saddened by the demise of the Goodgers
and determined that they should not be forgotten.

So, dipping a finger
into the pure white pool of Goodger memory,
he annointed the heads of the Badgers
who immediately gave up swearing and eating children.

And to this very day,
Badgers still wear the distinctive white mark
on their coats.          (As far as I know.)

# Beetle

What's that  t-i-c-k-i-n-g
you hear in the closet?

It's the stopwatch beetle
that docs it

It's timing
the dry rotting

In the old
wainscoting

And admiring
the eerie deposit.

# Blue Macaw

I used to keep a blue macaw
in my bedside bottom drawer

But he was never happy there
among my socks and underwear

He pined for sunshine, trees galore
as in Brazil and Ecuador

Knowing then what I must do
I journeyed south as far as Kew

In the Gardens set him free
(Wasn't that macawful of me?)

# Bookworms

Bookworms are the cleverest
of all the worms I know

While others meet their fate
on a fisherman's hook as bait

or churn out silk, chew up soil
or simply burn and glow

They make their homes in libraries
eating words to make them grow

In long-forgotten classics
latin tracts and dusty tomes

snug as bugs they hunker down
and set up family homes

Vegetarians mainly
they are careful what they eat

avoiding names of animals
or references to meat

They live to ripe old ages
and when its time to wend

they slip between the pages
curl up and eat 'The End'.

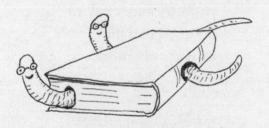

# Brushbaby

The Brushbaby
lives under the stairs

on a diet of dust
and old dog hairs

In darkness, dreading
the daily chores
of scrubbing steps
and kitchen floors

Dreaming of beauty
parlours and stardom
doomed to a life
of petty chardom.

# Budgerigars

Budgerigars
who smoke cigars

In the back
of large Rolls-Royces

Are mere poseurs
who put on airs

And seldom
have fine voices.

# Camel

The Sopwith camel
is worth a mention
as an economic
fuel-saving invention

Pump the hump
with gasoline, and lo!

It flies across the desert
in one go.

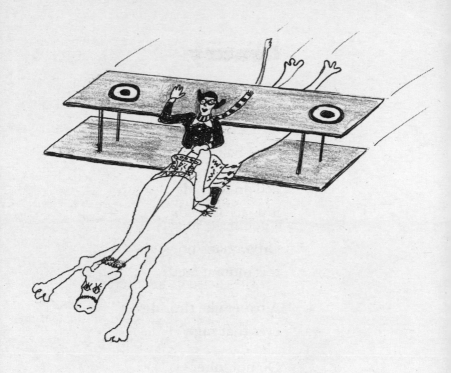

# Canary

Beware
the canary
gone hairy

Fed on steroids
instead of seeds

On humans now
this mutant feeds

A tweet like **thunder**
eyes that **rage**

Do not loiter
near its cage

Beware and be wary
There's nothing as scary
as a furry canary.

Who's a pretty boy then?

## Catapillow

A catapillow
is a useful pet

To keep
upon your bed

Each night you simply
fluff him up

Then rest
your weary head.

# Chimp

Ever see
a chimp
with a limp?

That's because
they keep to trees

Twisted ankles
and scraped knees

In Monkeydom
are rarities.

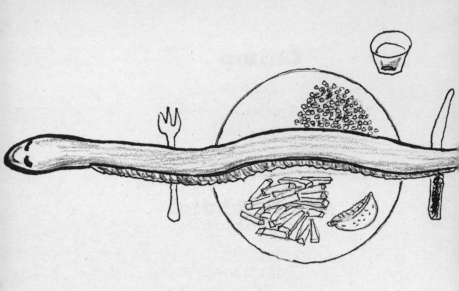

# Conger Eel

Is there
a    l o n g e r    meal
than a
conger eel?

# Dachshund

Ever see
a dachshund
dash under
lavatory doors?

Like a
limbo-dancer
(caught short)
on all fours.

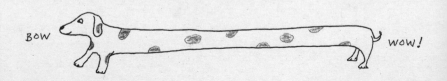

BOW        WOW!

# Dik-dik

Ever see
a dik-dik
being sick-sick?

That's because
they hic-hic
when eating leaves
too quick-quick

This antelope's
bad table manners
are the talk
of the savannas.

# Dingo

Ever heard
a dingo
sing? O
you should

A Thing
in darkness
gargling
blood.

# Doormouse

The doormouse
is seldom seen
except perhaps
at Halloween

The practical joker
of his genus
to grown-ups he's
a proper menace

The silly game
he likes to play
is banging on doors
then running away.

# Durianimal

The durianimal
is an amazing beast
(the word is Malaysian
for 'unusual feast')

Low in calories
and good to eat
an odd combination
half-fruit, half-meat

In taste and texture
beyond belief
imagine pineapple
and rare roast beef

(To vegetarians
they remain a puzzle
some refrain
while others guzzle)

Growing on trees
until mature
they drop from the branches
and crawl on the floor

With yellowish leaves
two legs and two arms
they live in the shade
of the durian palms

But not for long...
Considered such
a gourmet treat
their lives (like their bodies)
are short and sweet.

# Elephants

Ever see
elephants
with
smelly pants?

The answer:
potty-training
during
elephancy.

# Emus

To amuse
emus
on warm summer nights

Kiwis
do wiwis
from spectacular heights.

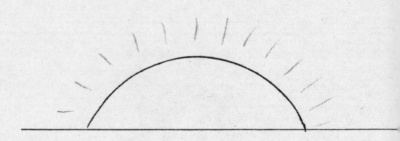

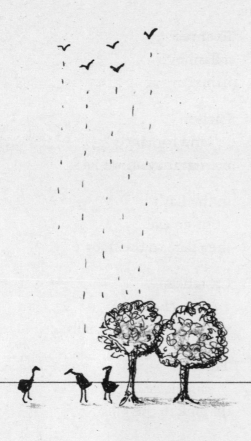

(In the skies above New Zealand
Kiwis once abounded.
But for health and safety reasons
For years now, they've been grounded.)

# Flamingo

Ever see
a flamingo
dance?

Passion
   and romance
is what they adore

In the flash
   of an eye
they take to the floor

Castanets
   they click
with a flick of their bills

Then
   *paso doble*
till pink in the gills

Flamingoes rule. Olé!

# Gibbon

Ever see
a baby gibbon
with a bib on?

Primates are prim
and surprisingly neat
when eating breakfast
with their feet.

# Goats

Duffle goats
cling to mountainsides
at heights
that make one boggle

And are hunted
by old beatniks
in search
of a long-lost toggle.

# Gorilla

Will a
gorilla
kill a
chinchilla?

No, because
they wouldn't dare
risk damaging the fur
of the rare and expensive
coats they wear.

# Grasshopper

Ever see
a grass hopper
in a
crashed chopper?

As pilots go
they are
far too skilled
to fly too low
and risk being killed.

# Grey Starling

Starlings
are brave things
and grey ones
the most

Like the
Grey Starling
rescuing sailors
off the
Northumbrian coast.

GRACE
DARLING
1815–42

# Haddock

Ever see
haddock
rock'n'roll?

Mad on
reggae
blues'n'soul

See them
shuffle
in a
soft-shoe shoal.

# Hamsters

Hamsters
built the dams
on the banks
of the Zuyder Zee

Beside which,
on Bank Hollandaise,
the whole dam nation
likes to be

Dads and their old dutches
(even kiddies in their prams)
give three hearty cheers
for the good old hamsterdams.

# Handfish

Handfish
are grand fish

they swim
about in pairs

hold each other
when they fall in love

and when
they say their prayers.

\* \* \*

They tickle
the sea's bare bottom

playful
as little kittens

and when
there's a nip in the ocean

wear brightly
coloured mittens.

# Hippos

Old hippos
one supposes
have terrible
colds in the noses

Attracted to these
nasal saunas
germs build their nests
in darkest corners

Then hang a sign
that says politely
(streaming, streaming,
day and nightly)

'Thank you for havin' us
in your nostrils so cavernous.'

# Lion

Never
rely on
a lion

To repay
the debt
that he owes

Androcles
was a
liar

As the lion
that ate him
well knows.

# Langoustine

A langoustine
would never be seen
on a plate with a
common shrimp

French and posh
it's superior nosh
though when peeled,
surprisingly limp.

# Lobster

Ever see
a lobster
dine with
a mobster?

The Crayfish
Twins did.

# Llama

Ever see
a llama
harm a
fly?

Not their
Kharma
that's why.

A Llama clock

# Loch Ness Monster

The Loch Ness Monster
Has just been spied
By a fisherman
Who almost died.

A dreadful thing, all scales and teeth
With sort of hairy bits beneath
(And that's only the fisherman!)

It lurks (the monster, i.e.)
In unfashionable depths under the sea
Swimming in and out of the loch
Through a tunnel cut deep in the rock.

A dozen sharks it eats for snacks
Octopie it loves to chew
Killer whales it breaks their backs
Is it true? Is it true?

Scottish folk don't easily scare
But most of them stay up in town
And only the very bravest dare
Sail alone when the sun goes down.

It swallowed an oil-rig in one gulp
Attacked a tanker and gobbled the crew
Battered a battleship into pulp
Is it true? Is it true?

I have a theory and I'll put it to you...

Any Scot worth his salt likes a wee dram of malt.
Out there fishing it's getting late
No one to talk to, only the bait
Nothing to do but drink and wait
And drink and drink, and drink and...wait!

Out of the mist like an Angel of Death
Comes howling a monster with brimstone breath
Gigantic serpent, satanic messiah,
The stench of an abattoir on fire.

Closer and closer upon the port bow
He tries to row but it's too late now
It rears above him jaws agape
Upturns the boat - a chance to escape?

Swimming madly like never before
He strikes out blindly and reaches the shore
Loses the boat but escapes with his life
(Well, that's the story he'd tell his wife).

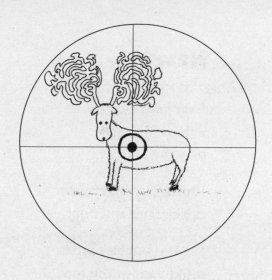

## Moose

Short-sighted hunters
choose moose

A target as large
as an orphanage wall

The quicker the trigger
the harder they fall

Short-sighted hunters
go home to their wives

Hang hats on the antlers
live short-sighted lives.

# Newt

Ever hear
a newt
play the flute?

Practising underwater
the classics and pop

See the bubbles burst
into music at the top.

# Nightingale

Ever spend
a night in jail
with
a nightingale?

When he sings
catch the notes
and string them together
squeeze through the bars
run hell for leather.

# Nits

the are
pits

# Osprey

Birds are feathered prayers
Offered up each day

To the Falconer upstairs
Let osprey.

# Ostrich

One morning
an ostrich
buried his head
   in the sand
and fell asleep

On waking
he couldn't remember
where he'd

      buried it.

# Oyster

Ever see an oyster
in a cloister?

Nuns in a shoal?

A monkfish praying
for a lost lemon sole?

# Peeve

Do you have any pet peeves?
*I have a pet peeve, his name is Spot*

Does he live on a strict diet?
*Yes, he loves his bowl of stricts*

Does he charge around the neighbourhood?
*About 50p an hour*

Is he housetrained?
*He occasionally peeves on the carpet*

Do you smack him?
*On the spot*

'out, damned Spot'

# Perch

Ever see
a perch
in church?

Every Sunday they pray
to keep the Big Bad
Fisherman at bay

Sad to say
that sometimes
when kneeling in a pew
in an uplifted state
the hook slips through
and they rise to the bait.

# Pigeon

A pigeon's
religion's
its own affair

Does God
have feathers?
Is St Peter's Square?

# Poodle

Ever eaten
poodle strudel?

It's sensational
with cream

I once had
chihuahua cheesecake

(Or was that
another bad dream?)

# Porcupine

A porcupine
that lost its quills
ran away from home
and took to the hills

All day long
it cried as it crawled
'No one can love
a creature so bald.'

But it was wrong.

A handsome kestrel
dropped by to say
'I Love You! I Love You!'
Then snatched it away.

pteroduckling

## Pterodactyl

Goodness gracious!
The pterodactyl
won't be back till
the next Cretaceous.

# Quokka

Why is
a quokka
cock-a-hoop?

Cos in Oz
there's no demand
for quokka soup.

# Rattlesnake

Ever see
a rattlesnake
wound around
a birthday cake?

Then go to
Colorado
where full of
bravado

Cowpokes
from the panhandles
blow out
the candles.

# Scallop

Ever see
a scallop

g a l l o p ?

Then go
to the track
at Ocean Bay

Where there's
sea-horse-racing
every day.

# Seagulls

Seagulls are eagles
with no head for heights

For soggy old crusts
they get into fights

Out-of-tune buskers
beggars and screechers

Seagulls are not
my favourite creatures.

# Sea-lion

Ever see
a sea-lion
make a bee-line
for a rose?

Then sneeze
with pollen
up its nose

It prefers
to freeze
on friendly floes.

# Shark

Ever see
a shark
picnic
in the park?

If he offers
you a bun

        Run!

# Skink

Ever see
a skink
on a
skating-rink?

Lizards
though
wizards
on dry brick walls
show a tendency
to upendency
resulting in falls.

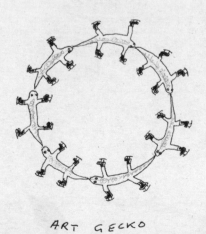

ART GECKO

# Slug

A 13-amp slug
you are likely to find
in the garden under a rock

Be careful
how you pick it up

You might get
a nasty shock.

# Sowester

A sowester
will keep you dry
when storms
toss the ship
that you're steering

But its squeals
will make you
want to cry
and wish
you were hard of hearing.

# Spider

Ever see
a hairy spider
hide inside
an airborne glider?

The pilot panics
on seeing what's in

As both of them
begin to spin.

# Squiggles.

Squiggles
love to draw
they are simply nuts about sketching

Doodling
in tree-top garrets
while squirrels do the fetching

Swapping
each little picture
for a pawful of food

(Although
charging extra
for Miss Nutkin in the nude.)

# Teapet

A teapet
I can recommend
to those who need
a loyal friend

Quiet, reliable
he'll never stray
content to sit
on his kitchen tray

Give him water
stroke his spout
say 't h a n k – y o u'
when the tea comes out.

# Terrapin

Ever see
a terrapin
bowling?

The pride
of the alley
is Dead-eye Sally

Another strike
hear the crowds cheer!

(A pity her run-up
takes over a year.)

# Unicorn

Ever see
a unicorn
one misty moisty
golden dawn
forlorn upon a garden lawn?

Oh yes.
Near the roccery I suppose
where the rocs live?

Beneath the tree
where the gryphons nest?

Beside the pool
where the mermaid
combs her hair?

Oh look!
Flying in over Sainsbury's
a squadron of dragons.

# War Thog

A war thog
is a mercenary beast

Who will show you
no mercy
until you're deceased

Armed to the teeth
with tusks
like scimitars

If you see one
give it
the widest perimeters.

# Water Bison

A
water bison
is what
yer wash
yer face in.

# Water Boatman

Said the Water Boatman
To the Water Boatmaid
'Won't you marry me?
We'll leave this boring pond behind
And sail across the sea.'

Said the Water Boatmaid
To the Water Boatman
'Thanks, but I've no wish
To leave my natural habitat
And feed the deep-sea fish.'

So the Water Boatman
Set off next day
To cross the ocean wide
Some say he lives on a tropical isle
Others say he died.

Said the Water Boatmaid
'How good to be free
And frail and pretty and young.'
And she sang a wee song
As she drifted along,

*And she didn't hear the snap*
*Of the dragonfly's tongue.*

*And she didn't hear the snap*
*Of the dragonfly's tongue.*

# Weasels

Weasels
at ease
at easels

Sables
at tables
tattoo

Hens'll kill
for pencils

And a cock'll
doodle too.

# Wombat

Ever see
a wombat
dressed
for combat?

By and large
his camouflage
is perfect

Khaki
from his head
to his toes

(Except for the helmet
which is orange, and glows!)

# Wordfish

Wordfish
    are swordfish
in a state of undress

Criss-crossing
    the ocean
in search of an S.

# Yak

Ever see
a yak
in a yashmak
that has shrunk

Ask for its
cash back
in a casbah
full of junk?

# Zonk

A zonk
one must conclude
is good for nothing
and very rude

Preferring
plonk to food
it drinks all day
until it's stewed

Then passes out.
Zonk.

**Roger McGough** is one of Britain's
best-loved poets, who also writes for the stage
and television. He has been awarded an OBE and
a CBE for services to poetry, and was recently
honoured with The Freedom of the City of Liverpool.
His many books for children include *Slapstick*,
*All the Best*, *Bad, Bad Cats*, and for Frances Lincoln,
*Dotty Inventions* and *Until I Met Dudley*. Called
"the patron saint of poetry" by the poet laureate
Carol Ann Duffy, Roger McGough gives readings
and performances all over the world.
He lives in London.

# MORE POETRY FROM
# FRANCES LINCOLN CHILDREN'S BOOKS

978-1-84780-167-8 • PB • £5.99

With wordplay and riddles, and poems that will make
you laugh, tell you stories and make you think, this is
a brilliant debut from an exciting new poet.

"A box of delights" – *Carol Ann Duffy*

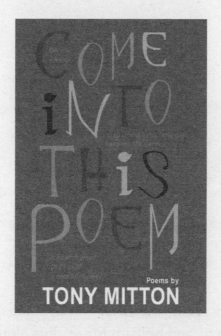

978-1-84780-169-2 • PB • £5.99

From spooky legends to dreamy poems, teasers
and rhymes, expect the unexpected. A poetry adventure
waiting to happen!

"A poet with a powerful feeling for story and language" –
*Carousel*

978-1-84780-168-5 • PB • £5.99

Perfect for younger children, these poems are fresh, funny and brilliant for reading aloud.

"These poems are born out of years of visiting infant classrooms. A real birthday party of words" – *Pie Corbett*